The Fisher Family
Beach Project

written by **Hollie Michaels**

illustrated by **Claudio Cerri**

PICTURE WINDOW BOOKS
a capstone imprint

Published by Picture Window Books, an imprint of Capstone
1710 Roe Crest Drive, North Mankato, Minnesota 56003
capstonepub.com

Copyright © 2025 by Capstone. All rights reserved. No part of this publication may be reproduced in whole or in part, or stored in a retrieval system, or transmitted in any form or by any means, electronic, mechanical, photocopying, recording, or otherwise, without written permission of the publisher.

Library of Congress Cataloging-in-Publication Data is available on the Library of Congress website.
ISBN: 9780756586621 (hardcover)
ISBN: 9780756586584 (paperback)
ISBN: 9780756586591 (ebook PDF)

Summary: It's beach day! And Golda and Ezra are looking forward to having a sandcastle-building competition with their friends. But when Ezra, Golda, and their parents arrive at the beach, things aren't pretty—there's trash everywhere. Can Golda, Ezra, their parents, and their friends save their beach day?

Editorial Credits
Editor: Ericka Smith; Designer: Sarah Bennett;
Production Specialist: Katy LaVigne

Any additional websites and resources referenced in this book are not maintained, authorized, or sponsored by Capstone. All product and company names are trademarks™ or registered® trademarks of their respective holders.

Table of Contents

Chapter 1
The Perfect Beach Day 5

Chapter 2
The Unexpected Mess 13

Chapter 3
The Big Cleanup 19

Meet Golda & Ezra's Family

Hi! I'm Golda Gene Fisher—GG, for short. I love to draw, sing, and roller-skate!

And I'm Ezra David Gomez. I'm Golda's stepbrother—and best friend! I love to play the trumpet, bake, and read.

And these are our parents.

Ima is our mom. She's a nurse. She speaks four languages—Hebrew, Spanish, English, and Yiddish!

Aba is our dad. He's a band teacher. He's always helping us figure out problems.

And this is Bagel and Lox! (They can only speak cat.)

Chapter 1

The Perfect Beach Day

Golda was the first one out of the car. "It's a perfect day for the beach!" she said.

Ima and Aba got out next. They unloaded buckets, blankets, and umbrellas and put them in their wagon.

Ezra slunk out of the car. Beach days meant sand *everywhere*. "Why do we need all this?" he asked.

"We're having a sandcastle contest, remember?" answered Golda. "We've got everything we need to win."

"I didn't know there'd be a winner," said Ezra, frowning.

Aba crossed his arms and pushed his eyebrows together. "Neither did I."

Golda copied Aba's pose. "The parents get to be the judges, so it's fair."

Aba and Ima looked at each other. They tried not to giggle.

But Golda noticed. She smiled brightly. Then she grabbed the wagon's arm. "Come on! Let's go!"

"Wait. Let's put on sunscreen first," said Ima.

Ima handed Ezra the sunscreen. If there's one thing Ezra hated more than sand in his hair, it was sunscreen on his face.

When he was done, he handed the bottle to Golda. She huffed. Then she smeared the white goo all over. When she was done, so was the bottle of sunscreen.

That's when Golda noticed there wasn't a recycling bin around. But she did see a trash can.

"Oy vey! It's overflowing," she said.

Aba looked around. His eyes widened. Garbage was spilling from *all* of the trash cans.

"Something's not right," said Ezra.

Chapter 2

The Unexpected Mess

When they got to the beach, Golda and Ezra saw their friends—Luis, Alejandro, Sabrina, and her little sister Laurel. They were all frowning.

"Look!" said Alejandro, pointing at the sand. Cans, wrappers, plastic bottles, and plastic bags were all over the place!

"We can't play here. It's gross," said Ezra.

"I really wanted to win the sandcastle contest!" said Laurel.

"Me too," said Golda.

Then a smile crept across Golda's face. She started to jump up and down and clap.

Ezra giggled. *"Golda's got an idea."*

"New plan," said Golda. "How about a different kind of contest?"

"I'm listening," said Luis.

"Why don't we race to pick up the trash?" Golda asked.

"Aba, don't you have trash bags in the car—from the cleanup you did with your band students?" asked Ezra.

"Yes! Gloves too!" said Aba and headed back to the car.

"What a perfect way to spend Tu BiShvat," said Ima.

"But isn't that the day we plant trees?" asked Ezra.

"Yes, but it's about taking care of our environment too," said Ima.

That got Golda thinking again. "Maybe it doesn't need to be a race."

"Yeah," said Sabrina. "Let's work together!"

Chapter 3

The Big Cleanup

Aba came back with trash bags and gloves. He passed them out.

Everyone got to work. Trash went in one bag, and things to recycle went in another.

Then something surprising happened. Other people on the beach came over to help.

"What a wonderful mitzvah!" said their neighbor Mrs. Rosenberg. "Hand me one of those bags."

About the Author

Hollie Michaels grew up in South Florida. She has lived in Miami, Chicago, Los Angeles, New York City, and London. Hollie works as an author, illustrator, theater teacher, and playwright. Many of her plays have been produced on stage. Her play *Children of Hooverville* is continually performed by middle school students around the country. Hollie lives in Connecticut with her husband, two kids, one corgi named Benny, and two cats—Oberon and Puck.

About the Illustrator

Claudio Cerri is an illustrator who lives and works in Stradella, a city in northern Italy. For more than 20 years, he has worked as an illustrator for the world's most important publishing houses. He's a lucky man because he has been able to turn his greatest passion into a beautiful job. His other passions are walking in nature, listening to music, reading, playing video games, and cuddling his cats.

Planting Project

Supplies

- old newspapers
- an empty can or yogurt container
- nontoxic paints
- paintbrushes
- potting soil
- seeds
- water

Steps

1. Create a spot to work by covering a table with old newspapers.
2. Paint the can or yogurt container. Be creative!
3. Let the can or container dry.
4. Fill the can or container with soil.
5. Press your finger about ½ inch into the soil. Drop one or two seeds into the hole. Then, cover the hole with soil.
6. Pour a little water on the soil where you planted the seeds.
7. Place the can or container in a sunny spot.
8. Check your plant every couple of days and water it if the soils feels dry.

Think About It!

1. How do you help take care of our environment? Do you recycle or compost? How about in your community? Make a list of how you can help keep your neighborhood clean.

2. Is there a spot near where you live that could use a cleanup? Whom would you ask to help? What supplies would you need? How long do you think it would take?

3. What does your perfect beach day look like? What would you bring to the beach? Draw everything you would bring on a piece of paper.

Learn Some Jewish Words

Jewish people speak many different languages, depending on where they live and where they are from. Some Ashkenazi Jews speak Yiddish. It's a language made from Hebrew, German, and other European languages. Sephardi Jews often speak Ladino, which comes from Spanish, Hebrew, Portuguese, Turkish, and Arabic. Mizrahi Jews usually speak Judeo-Arabic, a mix of Hebrew and Arabic.

Here are the words you read in this book:

aba (Hebrew: AH-bah)—father

Bal Tashchit (Hebrew: bah-ahl TAHSH-kheet)—a phrase that means "thou shalt not destroy" or "do not waste"

ima (Hebrew: EE-mah)—mother

mitzvah (Yiddish: MIHTZ-vuh)—a good deed

oy vey (Yiddish: oy VAY)—an expression that can mean many things, including you feel overwhelmed, frustrated, or surprised

Tu BiShvat (Hebrew: too beesh-VAHT)—a Jewish holiday known as the New Year of the Trees that's held on the 15th day of the Jewish month of Shevat

Celebrating Tu BiShvat

Tu BiShvat is a Jewish Earth Day—the Jewish New Year of the Trees. It is celebrated on the 15th day of the Jewish month Shevat. That's usually in January or February. It's a day when Jewish people plant and celebrate trees. But it is not just about planting and caring for trees—it's a day Jewish people celebrate and talk about the environment. Tu BiShvat reminds Jewish people to take care of the land and to work together to keep Earth clean.

It wasn't the beach day Golda had in mind, but it was still perfect.

"Are we done with the sand now?" Ezra asked as he shook his body like a puppy.

Golda giggled. *Well, almost perfect,* she thought.

Golda, Ezra, and their friends crowded around the sandcastle.

"Say 'Bal Tashchit!'" yelled Mrs. Rosenberg, holding up her phone to snap a picture.

"Bal Tashchit!" the kids screamed.

As they finished, Golda thought of something else. "Let's take a picture and make it into a sign. It can say, 'Keep our beach clean!'"

"Then," said Alejandro, "we can tape them to the trash cans!"

"Let's do it!" said Ezra.

They got to work building a giant sandcastle. Ima declared them all winners of the contest!

"I'm glad we cleaned up the beach," said Golda. "But I really wanted to build a sandcastle."

"Me too," said Luis.

That's when *Ezra* got an idea. "We still can! If we work together, we can build a great big one—and fast."

As they cleaned, Ezra spotted a seagull. Its head was stuck in a tattered bag.

"He needs help!" Ezra piped.

Aba and Ima gently removed the bag from the seagull's head.

"Is he alright?" asked Golda.

"He will be," said Ima.

The kids were relieved.

Everyone kept working until all the trash was picked up.